Fedge Makes a Wish!

Written and Illustrated by

JeFFrey Comanor

GO, GRACE!

For Grace
Welcome to the World!
Dr. Jeff
&
Fedge

1-16-00

Turner Publishing, Inc.
ATLANTA

Somewhere in the great blue ocean, on a faraway island called Dandy...

there lived a friendly
dragon named Fedge.

Fedge wished he was a flying dragon. Sometimes he would sing about flying.

He would even dream about it.

Most of the time Fedge was very happy. He and his friends, Snord and Huff, would play and enjoy every day that came along.

But every now and then, they would
have to hide in the jungle from the
Great Hairy
Condor Snooch.

It wasn't so much that
the Snooch was really
bad. He just had a
terrible habit of picking
things up from one place
and putting them
down in another.

And even worse than that, he'd forget where he put them, so he couldn't put them back!

(Maybe you know someone like the Snooch.)

One day Fedge
was walking on the beach,
and he saw a giant
storm cloud
headed straight
for Dandy Island!

At first
the wind
was not
too strong.

It only
picked up
a few leaves.

Then the
trees began
to bend low.

And soon things were flying through the air!

In fact, the wind was so strong that you would have to hold on to something to keep from being blown away!

(So would I!)

Fedge hung on for all he was worth. As he was hanging on to

the tree, he saw the Snooch
take off into the wind.

Suddenly, a **big, scary wave** jumped up.

The wave caught the Snooch by surprise.

It knocked the Snooch into
the water, and that's
when he found out
he couldn't swim!

(Actually, he had never tried before.)

Fedge thought to himself, "Someone has got to help that poor Snooch."

He crawled to a fallen branch and pushed it into the stormy water.

At first, Fedge could hardly get anywhere in the wild waves.

But he wouldn't quit, and soon he was on his way to save the Snooch.

The Snooch grabbed hold of
the branch, and together
Fedge and the Snooch fought
their way back to shore.

When they were safe,
the Snooch said two words
he had never said before.
"Thank You."

"You saved me," said the Snooch. "You are my first real friend. There is something I want to do for you."

And with that, the Snooch flew away.

Fedge waited...

and waited...

and waited.

One day, not too much later,
Fedge saw a red dot in the sky

Do you know what it was?

Guess!

You are right!
It was the Great Snooch, returning to Dandy Island.

The Snooch was smudged with smoke, and around his neck was a strange little pouch.

The Snooch said, "I've been to an island where dragons live. On that island is a great volcano, and at the very top, there's magic dust that comes from the fire within. It's called dragon dust, and it has the power to make a dragon's wish come true."

As the Snooch sprinkled the magic dragon dust over him, Fedge wished very hard.

He said, "I wish I had wings like the Snooch."

Suddenly an amazing thing began to happen. Little bumps began to grow on Fedge's shoulders.

They grew...

and they grew...

Until they were wonderful, big wings.

Fedge couldn't believe his eyes.

He began to flap his wings faster and faster.

Suddenly Fedge was in the air.

He climbed, he swooped, he hovered,

and he even flew upside down!

It was a glorious day on Dandy Island! The Snooch had new friends. Snord and Huff didn't have to hide because the Snooch was too busy having fun to carry anything off. And as for Fedge...

It was the happiest day of his life!

...and by the way, this one's for Faye, too!

COPYRIGHT © 1996 BY JEFFREY M. COMANOR

"EVERY DRAGON NEEDS SOME WINGS" BY PERMISSION COMANOR MUSIC, INC.

PUBLISHED BY TURNER PUBLISHING, INC.

A SUBSIDIARY OF TURNER BROADCASTING SYSTEM, INC.

1050 TECHWOOD DRIVE, N.W.

ATLANTA, GEORGIA 30318

DISTRIBUTED BY ANDREWS AND MCMEEL

A UNIVERSAL PRESS SYNDICATE COMPANY

4900 MAIN STREET

KANSAS CITY, MISSOURI 64112

FIRST EDITION 10 9 8 7 6 5 4 3 2 1

ISBN 1-57036-356-0

EDITOR: DEE ANN GRAND

DESIGN & ART DIRECTION: MICHAEL J. WALSH

PRODUCTION: ANNE MURDOCH

PRINTED IN HONG KONG